THE WRECKERS OF SABLE ISLAND

J. MACDONALD OXLEY

THE WRECKERS OF SABLE ISLAND

CHAPTER I.

THE SETTING FORTH.

A voyage across the Atlantic Ocean in the year 1799 was not the every-day affair that it has come to be at the present time. There were no "ocean greyhounds" then. The passage was a long and trying one in the clumsy craft of those days, and people looked upon it as a more serious affair than they now do on a tour round the world.

In the year 1799 few people thought of travelling for mere pleasure. North, south, east, and west, the men went on missions of discovery, of conquest, or of commerce; but the women and children abode at home, save, of course, when they ventured out to seek new homes in that new world which was drawing so many to its shores.

It was therefore not to be wondered at that the notion of Eric Copeland going out to his father in far-away Nova Scotia should form the subject of more than one family council at Oakdene Manor, the beautiful country seat of the Copeland family, situated in one of the prettiest parts of Warwickshire.

Eric was the only son of Doctor Copeland, surgeon-in-chief of the Seventh Fusiliers, the favourite regiment of the Duke of Kent, the father of Queen Victoria. This regiment formed part of the garrison at Halifax, then under the command of the royal duke himself; and the doctor had written to say that if the squire, Eric's grandfather, approved, he would like Eric to come out to him, as his term of service had been extended three years beyond what he expected, and he wanted to have his boy with him. At the same time, he left the matter entirely in the squire's hands for him to decide.

So far as the old gentleman was concerned, he decided at once.

"Send the boy out there to that wild place, and have him scalped by an Indian or gobbled by a bear before he's there a month? Not a bit of it. I won't hear of it. He's a hundred times better off here."

The squire, be it observed, held very vague notions about Nova Scotia, and indeed the American continent generally, in spite of his son's endeavours to enlighten him. He still firmly believed that there were as many wigwams as houses in New York, and that Indians in full war-paint and plumes were every day seen on the streets of Philadelphia; while as for poor little Nova Scotia, it was more than his mind could take in how the Duke of Kent could ever bring himself to spend a week in such an outlandish place, not to speak of a number of years.

So soon as Eric learned of his father's request, he was not less quick in coming to a conclusion, but it was of a precisely opposite kind to the squire's. He was what the Irish would call "a broth of a boy." Fifteen last birthday, five feet six inches in height, broad of shoulder and stout of limb, yet perfectly proportioned, as nimble on his feet as a squirrel, and as quick of eye as a king-bird, entirely free from any trace of nervousness or timidity, good-looking in that sense of the word which means more than merely handsome, courteous in his manners, and quite up to the mark in his books, Eric represented the best type of the British boy as he looked about him with his brave brown eyes, and longed to be something more than simply a school-boy, and to see a little of that great world up and down which his father had been travelling ever since he could remember.

"Of course I want to go to father," said he, promptly and decidedly. "I don't believe there are any bears or Indians at Halifax; and even if there should be, I don't care. I'm not afraid of them."

He had not the look of a boy that could be easily frightened, or turned aside from anything upon which he had set his heart, and the old squire felt as though he were seeing a youthful reflection of himself in the sturdy spirit of resolution shown by his grandson.

"But, Eric, lad," he began to argue, "whether the Indians and bears are plentiful or not, I don't see why you want to leave Oakdene, and go away out to a wild place that is only fit for soldiers. You're quite happy with us here, aren't you?" And the old gentleman's face took on rather a reproachful expression as he put the question.

Eric's face flushed crimson, and crossing over to where the squire sat, he bent down and kissed his wrinkled forehead tenderly.

"I am quite happy, grandpa. You and grandma do so much for me that it would be strange if I wasn't. But you know I have been more with you than I have with my own father; and now when he wants me to go out to him, I want to go too. You can't blame me, can you?"

What Eric said was true enough. The doctor's regiment had somehow come in for more than its share of foreign service. It had carried its colours with credit over the burning plains of India, upon the battle-fields of the Continent, and then, crossing to America, had taken its part, however ineffectually, in the struggle which ended so happily in the birth of a new nation. During all of his years Eric had remained at Oakdene, seeing nothing of his father save when he came to them on leave for a few months at a time.

These home-comings of the doctor were the great events in Eric's life. Nothing was allowed to interfere with his enjoyment of his father's society. All studies were laid aside, and one day of happiness followed another, as together they rode to hounds, whipped the trout-streams, shot over the coverts where pheasants were in plenty, or went on delightful excursions to lovely places round about the neighbourhood.

Dr. Copeland enjoyed his release from the routine of military duty quite as much as Eric did his freedom from school, and it would not have been easy to say which of the two went in more heartily for a good time.

It was just a year since the doctor had last been home on leave, and a year seems a very long time to a boy of fifteen, so that when the letter came proposing that Eric should go out to his father (it should have been told before that his mother was dead, having been taken away from him when he was a very little fellow), and spend three long years with him without a break, if the doctor had been in Kamtchatka or Tierra del Fuego instead of simply in Nova Scotia, Eric would not have hesitated a moment, but have jumped at the offer.

The old squire was very loath to part with his grandson, and it was because he knew it would be so that the doctor had not positively asked for Eric to be sent out, but had left the question to be decided by the squire.

Perhaps Eric might have failed to carry his point but for the help given him by Major Maunsell, a brother-officer of Doctor Copeland's, who had been home on leave, and in whose charge Eric was to be placed if it was decided to let him go.

The major had come to spend a day or two at Oakdene a little while before taking his leave of England, and of course the question of Eric's returning to Nova Scotia with him came up for discussion. Eric pleaded his case very earnestly.

"Now please listen to me a moment," said he, taking advantage of a pause in the conversation. "I love you, grandpa and grandma, very dearly, and am very happy with you here; but I love my father too, and I never see him, except just for a little while, when he comes home on leave, and it would be lovely to be with him all the time for three whole years. Besides that, I do want to see America, and this is such a good chance. I am nearly sixteen now, and by the time father gets back I'll have to be going to college, and then, you know, he says he's going to leave the army and settle down here, so that dear knows when I can ever get the chance to go again. Oh! please let me go, grandpa, won't you?"

Major Maunsell's eyes glistened as he looked at Eric and listened to him. He was an old bachelor himself, and he could not help envying Doctor Copeland for his handsome, manly son. At once he entered into full sympathy with him in his great desire, and determined to use all his influence in supporting him.

"There's a great deal of sense in what the boy says," he remarked. "It is such a chance as he may not get again in a hurry. There's nothing to harm him out in Halifax; and his father is longing to have him, for he's always talking to me about him, and reading me bits out of his letters."

So the end of it was that the major and Eric between them won the day, and after taking the night to think over it, the good old squire announced the next morning at breakfast that he would make no further objections, and that Eric might go.

The troop-ship in which Major Maunsell was going would sail in a week, so there was no time to be lost in getting Eric ready for the voyage, and for the long sojourn in the distant colony. Many were the trunks of clothing, books, and other things that had to be packed with greatest care, and their number would have been doubled if the major had not protested against taking the jams, jellies, pickles, medicines, and other domestic comforts that the loving old couple wanted Eric to take with him, because they felt sure he could get nothing so good out in Halifax.

All too quickly for them the day came when they were to say good-bye to their grandson, and the parting was a very tearful and trying one. Full of joy as Eric felt, he could not keep back the tears when his white-haired grandmother hugged him again and again to her heart, exclaiming fervently,—

"God bless and keep my boy! May his almighty arms be underneath and round about you, my darling. Put your trust in him, Eric, no matter what may happen."

And the bluff old squire himself was suspiciously moist about the eyes as the carriage drove away and Eric was really off to Chatham in charge of Major Maunsell, with whom he had by this time got to be on the best of terms.

At Chatham they found their ship in the final stage of preparation for the voyage. They were to sail in the *Francis*, a fine, fast gun-brig of about three hundred tons, which had in her hold a very valuable cargo, consisting of the Duke of Kent's library, together with a quantity of very costly furniture, precious wines, and other luxuries intended to make as comfortable as possible the lot of his royal highness in the garrison at Halifax. The major and Eric were assigned a roomy cabin to themselves, in which they at once proceeded to make themselves at home.

During the few days that intervened before the sailing of the *Francis*, Eric's enjoyment of the novel scenes around him could hardly be put into words. All he knew about the sea was what he had learned from a summer now and then at a watering-place; and the great gathering of big ships at Chatham; the unceasing bustle as some came in from long voyages and others went forth to take their places upon distant stations; the countless sailors and dock-hands swarming like ants hither and thither; the important-looking officers strutting about in gold-laced coats, and calling out their commands in such hoarse tones that Eric felt tempted to ask if they all had very bad colds; the shrill sound of the boatswains' whistles that seemed to have no particular meaning; the martial music of bands playing apparently for no other reason than just because they wanted to,—all this made up a wonder-world for Eric in which he found a great deal of delight.

There was just one cloud upon his happiness. Among his many pets at Oakdene his special favourite was a splendid mastiff that the squire had given him as a birthday present two years before. Prince was a superb animal, and devoted to his young master. No sooner had it been settled that Eric should go out to his father than the boy at once asked if his dog might not go with him. Major Maunsell had no objection himself, but feared that the captain of the *Francis* would not hear of it. However, he thought that Eric might bring the dog up to Chatham, and then if the captain would not let him on board he could be sent back to Oakdene.

Prince accordingly accompanied him, and a place having been found for him with a friend of the major's, his master had no peace of mind until the question was settled. Some days passed before he got a chance to see Captain Reefwell, who was, of course, extremely busy; but at last he managed to catch him one day just after lunch, when he seemed in a pretty good humour, and without wasting time preferred his request, trembling with eager hope as he did so. The gruff old sailor at first bluntly refused him; but Eric bravely returning to the charge, his kind heart was moved to the extent of making him say,—

"Well, let me have a look at your dog, anyway."

Hoping for the best, Eric ran off and returned with Prince. Captain Reefwell scanned the noble animal critically, and stretched out his hand to pat him, whereupon the mastiff gravely lifted his right paw and placed it in the captain's horny palm.

"Shiver my timbers! but the dog's got good manners," said the captain in surprise. "Did you teach him that?" turning to Eric.

"Yes, sir," replied Eric proudly; "and he can do other things too." And he proceeded to put the big dog through a number of tricks which pleased the old sailor so much that finally he said, with a smile,—

"All right, my lad. You may bring your dog on board. But, mind you, he comes before the mast. He's not a cabin passenger."

"Oh, thank you, sir! thank you, sir!" cried Eric joyfully.—"I won't let you in the cabin, will I, Prince? Isn't it splendid? You're to come with me after all." And he hugged the mastiff as though he had been his own brother.

CHAPTER II.

IN ROUGH WEATHER.

It was the first of November when the *Francis* got off, and Captain Reefwell warned his passengers that they might expect a rather rough voyage, as they were sure to have a storm or two in crossing at that time of year. Eric protested that he would not mind; he was not afraid of a storm. Indeed, he wanted to see one really good storm at sea, such as he had often read about.

But he changed his tune when the *Francis* began to pitch and toss in the chops of the English Channel, and with pale face and piteous voice he asked the major "if a real storm were worse than this." A few days later, however, when he got his sea-legs all right, and the *Francis* was bowling merrily over the broad Atlantic before a favouring breeze, his courage came back to him, and he felt ready for anything.

The *Francis* was not more than a week out before the captain's prediction began to be fulfilled. One storm succeeded another with but little rest between, the wind blowing from all quarters in turn. Driven hither and thither before it, the *Francis* struggled gallantly toward her destination. So long as he was out in mid-Atlantic Captain Reefwell seemed quite indifferent to the boisterous weather. He told his passengers that he was sorry for the many discomforts they were forced to endure, but otherwise showed no concern. He was a daring sailor, and had crossed the ocean a score of times before. As they approached the American side, however, and the storm still continued, he grew very anxious, as his troubled countenance and moody manner plainly showed. The truth was that he had been driven out of his course, and had lost his reckoning, owing to sun and stars alike having been invisible for so many days. He had no clear idea of his distance from the coast, and unless he could soon secure a satisfactory observation the*Francis* would be in a perilous plight.

The first of December was marked by a storm more violent than any which had come before, followed by a dense fog which swathed the ship in appalling gloom. The captain evidently regarded this fog as a very grave addition to his difficulties. He hardly left the quarter-deck, and his face grew haggard and his eyes bloodshot with being constantly on the look-out. Realizing that a crisis was at hand, and determined to know the worst, Major Maunsell made bold to ask the captain to tell him the real state of affairs. Captain Reefwell hesitated for a moment, then muttering something about "might as well out with it," he laid his hand upon the major's shoulder, and looking straight into his eyes, with a strange expression of sympathy, said in his gravest tones,—

"Major, it's just this: unless I'm clean lost, we must now be somewhere near Sable Island. I'm expecting to hear the roar of its breakers any minute, and once the *Francis* gets amongst them, God help us all! Sable Island makes sure work." And he turned away abruptly, as though to hide his feelings.

Captain Reefwell's words sent a shudder straight and swift through Major Maunsell's heart. The latter already knew of the bad reputation of that strange island which scarcely lifts itself above the level of the Atlantic, less than a hundred miles due east from Nova Scotia. Stories that chilled the blood had from time to time floated up to Halifax—stories of shipwreck following fast upon shipwreck, and no one surviving to tell the tale.

But even more appalling than the fury of the storm that scourged the lonely island were the deeds said to be done by monsters in human guise who plied the wrecker's trade there, and, acting upon the principle that dead men tell no tales, had made it their care to put out of the way all whom even the cruel billows had spared.

With a heavy heart the major made his way back to the cabin, where he found Eric, upon whose bright spirits the long and stormy voyage had told heavily, looking very unhappy as he tried to amuse himself with a book. The boy was worn out by the ceaseless pitching and tossing of the vessel. He felt both home-sick and sea-sick, as indeed did many another of the passengers, who with one accord were wishing themselves safely upon land again. He looked up eagerly as the major entered.

"What does the captain say, major?" he asked, his big brown eyes open their widest. "Will the storm soon be over, and are we near Halifax?"

Concealing his true feelings, the major replied with well-put-on cheerfulness,—

"The captain says that if this fog would only lift, and let him find out exactly where we are, Eric, he would be all right. There is nothing to do but to wait, and hope for the best." And sitting down beside Eric, he threw his arm about him in a tender, protecting way that showed how strongly he felt.

So intense was the anxiety on board the *Francis* that none of the passengers thought of going to their berths or taking off their clothes that night, but all gathered in the cabins, finding what cheer and comfort they could in one another's company.

In the main cabin were other officers besides Major Maunsell—namely, Captain Sterling of the Fusiliers, Lieutenant Mercer of the Royal Artillery, and Lieutenants Sutton, Roebuck, and Moore of the 16th Light Dragoons; while in the fore-cabin were household servants of the prince and soldiers of the line, bringing the total number of passengers up to two hundred.

During the night Captain Reefwell, seeing that it was no longer any use to conceal the seriousness of the situation, sent word to all on board to prepare for the worst, as the ship might be among the breakers at any moment. The poor passengers hastened to gather their most precious possessions into little bundles, and to prepare themselves for the approaching struggle with death.

The night wore slowly on, the sturdy brig straining and groaning as the billows made a plaything of her, tossing her to and fro as though she was no heavier than a chip, while the fierce storm shrieked through the rigging in apparent glee at having so rich a prize for the wreckers of Sable Island.

It was a brave band that awaited its fate in the main cabin. The men were borne up by the dauntless fortitude of the British soldier, and, catching their spirit, Eric manifested a quiet courage well worthy of the name he bore. He had Prince with him now, for the captain had himself suggested that he had better have the dog near at hand. The noble creature seemed to have some glimmering of their common peril, for he kept very close to his young master, and every now and then laid his huge head upon Eric's knee and looked up into his face with an expression that said as plainly as words,—

"Nothing but death can ever part us. You can depend upon me to the very uttermost."

And hugging him fondly, Eric answered,—

"Dear old Prince! You'll help me if we are wrecked, won't you?" at which Prince wagged his tail responsively, and did his best to lick his master's face.

Now and then some one would creep up on deck, and brave the fury of the blast for a few moments, in hope of finding some sign of change for the better; and on his return to the cabin the others would eagerly scan his countenance and await his words, only to be met with a sorrowful shake of the head that rendered words unnecessary.

Eric alone found temporary forgetfulness in sleep. He was very weary, and, though fully alive to the danger so near at hand, could not keep from falling into a fitful slumber, as he lay upon the cushioned seat that encircled the cabin, Prince stationing himself at his side and pillowing his head in his lap.

Poor Prince was by no means so handsome a creature now as when his good looks and good manners won the captain's heart. The long stormy passage had been very hard upon him. He had grown gaunt, and his smooth, shiny skin had become rough and unkempt. Otherwise, however, he was not much the worse, and was quite ready for active duty if his services should be needed.

Awaking from a light sleep, in which he dreamed that he and Prince were having a glorious romp on the lawn at Oakdene, which somehow seemed to be undulating in a very curious fashion, Eric caught sight of Major Maunsell returning to the cabin after a visit to the upper deck, and at once ran up to him and plied him with eager questions.

"Is the storm getting any better, and will it soon be daylight again?"

The major did his best to look cheerful as he answered,—

"Well, the storm is no worse, Eric, at all events, and it will not be long before daylight comes."

"But even if we should be wrecked," said Eric, looking pleadingly into the major's face, "we might all get ashore all right, mightn't we? I've often read of shipwrecks in which everybody was saved."

"Certainly, my boy, certainly," replied the major promptly, although deep down in his heart he seemed to hear Captain Reefwell's ominous words, "Sable Island makes sure work."

"And, major," continued Eric, "I'm going to keep tight hold of Prince's collar if we do get wrecked. He can swim ever so much better than I can, and he'll pull me ashore all right, won't he?"

"That's a capital idea of yours, my boy," said the major, smiling tenderly upon him. "Keep tight hold of Prince, by all means. You couldn't have a better life-preserver."

"I don't want to be wrecked, that's certain; but if we are, I'm very glad I've got Prince here to help me—the dear old fellow that he is!" And so saying, Eric threw himself down upon his dog and gave him a hearty hug, which the mastiff evidently much enjoyed. Day broke at last, if the slow changing of the thick darkness into a dense gray fog could rightly be called daybreak.

The *Francis* still bravely battled with the tempest. She had proved herself a trusty ship, and, with Captain Reefwell on the quarter-deck, more than a match for the worst fury of wind and wave.

But no ship that ever has been or ever will be built could possibly pass through the ordeal of the Sable Island breakers, whose awful thunder might at any moment be heard above the howling of the blast. At breakfast-time the worn and weary passengers gathered around the table for what would, in all probability, be their last meal on board the *Francis*, and perhaps their last on earth. The fare was not very tempting, for what could the cooks do under such circumstances? But the passengers felt no disposition to complain. Indeed, they had little appetite to eat, and were only making a pretence of doing so, when a sailor burst into the cabin, his bronzed face blanched with fear, as he shouted breathlessly,—

"Captain says for all to come up on deck. The ship will strike in a minute."

Instantly there was wild confusion and a mad rush for the companion-way; but Major Maunsell waited to take Eric's hand tightly into his before pressing on with the others. When they reached the deck an awful scene met their eyes. The fog had lifted considerably, so that it was possible to see some distance from the ship; and there, right across her bows, not more than a quarter of a mile away, a tremendous line of breakers stretched as far as eye could see.

Straight into their midst the *Francis* was helplessly driving at the bidding of the storm-fiend. No possible way of escape! Not only did the breakers extend to right and left until they were lost in the shifting fog, but the nearest line was evidently only an advance-guard; for beyond it other lines, not less formidable, could be dimly descried, rearing their snowy crests of foam as they rolled fiercely onward.

"Heaven help us!" cried Major Maunsell, as with one swift glance he took in the whole situation; and drawing Eric close to him, he made his way through the confusion to the foot of the main-mast, which offered a secure hold for the time being.

A few minutes later the *Francis* struck the first bar with a shock that sent everybody who had not something to hold on to tumbling upon the deck. But for the major's forethought, both he and Eric might at that moment have been borne off into the boiling surges; for a tremendous billow rushed upon the helpless vessel, sweeping her from stern to stem, and carrying away a number of the soldiers, who, having nothing to hold on by, were picked up like mere chips of wood and hurried to their doom. Their wild cries for the help that could not be given them pierced the ears of the others, who did not know but that the next billow would treat them in like manner.

Again and again was the ill-starred ship thus swept by the billows, each time fresh victims falling to their fell fury. Then came a wave of surpassing size, which, lifting the *Francis* as though she had been a mere feather, bore her over the bar into the deeper water beyond. Here, after threatening to go over upon her beam-ends, she righted once more, and drove on toward the next bar.

CHAPTER III.

THE WRECK.

Major Maunsell gave a great gasp of relief when the brig righted.

"Keep tight hold of your rope, Eric," he cried encouragingly. "Please God, we may reach shore alive yet."

Drenched to the skin and shivering with cold, Eric held tightly on to the rope with his right hand and to Prince's collar with his left. Prince had crouched close to the foot of the mast, and the waves swept by him as though he had been carved in stone.

"All right, sir," Eric replied, as bravely as he could. "It's pretty hard work, but I'll not let go."

Rearing and plunging amid the froth and foam, the *Francis* charged at the second bar, struck full upon it with a force that would have crushed in the bow of a less sturdy craft, hung there for a few minutes while the breakers, as if greedy for their prey, swept exultantly over her, and then, responding to the impulse of another towering wave, leaped over the bar into the deeper water beyond.

But she could not stand much more of such buffeting, for she was fast becoming a mere hulk. Both masts had gone by the board at the last shock, and poor little Eric certainly would have gone overboard with the main-mast but for his prompt rescue by the major from the entangling rigging.

"You had a narrow escape that time, Eric," said the major, as he dragged the boy round to the other side of the mast, where he was in less danger.

The passage over the bars having thus been effected, the few who were still left on board the *Francis* began to cherish hopes of yet reaching the shore alive.

Between the bars and the main body of the island was a heavy cross-sea, in which the brig pitched and tossed like a bit of cork. Somewhere beyond this wild confusion of waters was the surf which broke upon the beach itself, and in that surf the final struggle would take place. Whether or not a single one of the soaked, shivering beings clinging to the deck would survive it, God alone knew. The chances of their escape were as one in a thousand—and yet they hoped.

There were not many left now. Captain Sterling was gone, and Lieutenants Mercer and Sutton. Besides the major and Eric, only Lieutenants Roebuck and Moore of the cabin passengers were still to be seen. Of the soldiers and crew, almost all had been swept away; but Captain Reefwell still held to his post upon the quarter-deck by keeping tight hold to a belaying-pin.

The distance between the bars and the beach was soon crossed, and the long line of foaming billows became distinct through the driving mist.

"Don't lose your grip on Prince, my boy," called the major to Eric. "We'll strike in a second, and then—"

But before he could finish the sentence the ship struck the beach with fearful force, and was instantly buried under a vast mountain of water that hurled itself upon her as though it had long been waiting for the chance to destroy her. When the billow had spent its force, the decks were clear. Not a human form was visible where a moment before more than a score of men had been clinging for dear life. Hissing and seething like things of life, and sending their spray and spume high into the mist-laden air, the merciless breakers bore their victims off to cast them contemptuously upon the beach. Then, ere they could scramble ashore, they would be caught up again and carried off by the recoil of the wave, to be once more dashed back as though they were the playthings of the water.

The major and Eric were separated in the wild confusion; but Eric was not parted from Prince. About his brawny neck the mastiff wore a stout leathern collar, and to this Eric clung with a grip that not even the awful violence of the breakers could unloose. Rather did it make his sturdy fingers but close the tighter upon the leathern band.

Into the boiling flood the boy and dog were plunged together, and bravely they battled to make the shore. The struggle would be a tremendous one for them, and the issue only too doubtful. The slope of the beach was very gradual, and there was a long distance between where the brig struck and the dry land. Wholly blinded and half-choked by the driving spray, Eric could do nothing to direct his course. But he could have had no better pilot than the great dog, whose unerring instinct pointed him straight to the shore.

How long they struggled with the surf Eric could not tell. But his strength had failed, and his senses were fast leaving him, when his feet touched something firmer than tossing waves, and presently he and Prince were lifted up, and then hurled violently upon the sand. Had he been alone, the recoil of the wave would certainly have carried him back again into the surge; but the dog dug his big paws into the soft beach, and forced his way up, dragging his master with him.

Dizzy, bewildered, and faint, Eric staggered to his feet, looked about him in hope of finding the major near, and then, seeing nobody, fell forward upon the sand in a dead faint.

How long he lay unconscious upon the beach Eric had no idea; but when he at length came to himself, he found a big, bushy-bearded man bending over him with a half-pitying, half-puzzled look, while beside him, ready for a spring, was faithful Prince, regarding him with a look that said as plainly as words,—

"Attempt to do my master any harm and I will be at your throat."

But the big man seemed to have no evil intent. He had evidently been waiting for Eric to gain consciousness, and as soon as the boy opened his eyes, said in a gruff but not unkind voice,—-

"So you're not dead after all, my hearty. More's the pity, maybe. Old Evil-Eye'll be wanting to make a clean job of it, as usual."

Eric did not at all take in the meaning of the stranger's words; his senses had not yet fully returned. He felt a terrible pain in his head and a distressing nausea, and when he tried to get upon his feet he found the effort too much for him. He fell back with a cry of pain that made the affectionate mastiff run up to him and gently lick his face, as though to say,—

"What's the matter, dear master? Can I do anything for you?"

The man then seemed, for the first time, to take notice of the dog, and putting forth a huge, horny hand, he patted him warily, muttering under his beard,—

"Sink me straight, but it's a fine beast. I'll have him for my share, if I have to take the boy along with him."

Perceiving by some subtle instinct the policy of being civil, Prince permitted himself to be patted by the stranger, and then lay down again beside him in a manner that betokened, "When wanted, I'm ready."

Eric was eager to hear about Major Maunsell and the others who had been on board the *Francis*. Were it not for his weakness he would be running up and down the beach in search of them. But the terrible struggle with the surf, following upon the long exposure to the storm, had completely exhausted him, and he was sorely bruised besides. Turning his face up to the strange man, who seemed to have nothing further to say on his own account, he asked him anxiously,—

"Where's Major Maunsell? Is he all right?"

Instead of answering, the man looked away from Eric, and there was an expression on his face that somehow sent a chill of dread to the boy's heart.

"Please tell me what has happened. Oh, take me to him, won't you? He's looking after me, you know," he pleaded earnestly, the tears beginning to well from his eyes.

Still the big man kept silence. Then as Eric pressed him with entreaty, he suddenly wheeled about and spoke in gruffer tones than he had so far used,—

"You'd best be still and keep quiet. You'll never see Major Maunsell, as you call him, or any of the rest of them again, and you might just as well know it first as last."

At these dreadful words Eric raised himself by a great effort to a sitting posture, gazed into the man's face as though hoping to find some sign of his not being in earnest, and then with a cry of frantic grief flung himself back and buried his face in his hands, while his whole frame shook with the violence of his sobbing.

The man stood watching him in silence, although his face, hard and stern as it was, gave evidence of his being moved to sympathy with the boy. He seemed to be thinking deeply, and to be in much doubt as to what he should do. He was just about to stoop down and lift Eric up, when a harsh, grating voice called out,—

"Hallo, Ben! What have you got there?"

CHAPTER IV.

ALONE AMONG STRANGERS.

Ben started as though he had been caught at some crime, and there was a sulky tone in his voice that showed very plainly that he resented the appearance of the questioner, as he replied,—

"Only a boy and a dog."

The other man drew near and inspected Eric closely. Prince at once sprang to his feet, and taking up his position between the new-comer and his young master, fixed his big eyes upon the former, while his teeth showed threateningly, and a deep growl issued from between them.

It was no wonder that the sagacious mastiff's suspicions were aroused, for surely never before had his eyes fallen upon so sinister a specimen of humanity. The man was of little more than medium height; but his frame showed great strength, combined with unusual activity, and one glance was sufficient to mark him out as a man with whom few could cope. His countenance, naturally ugly, had been the playground of the strongest and coarsest passions that degrade humanity, and was rendered still more hideous by the loss of his left eye, which had been gouged out in a drunken *mêlée*, and by a frightful scar that ran clear from temple to chin on the right side of his face. Through the remaining eye all the vile nature of the man found expression, and its baleful glare, when fixed full upon one, was simply appalling.

To it, perhaps more than to any other quality, Evil-Eye—for so his comrades appropriately nicknamed him—owed his influence among them; for he was, in some sort, regarded as a leader of the band of wreckers to which both he and Ben belonged.

Evil-Eye held in his right hand a cutlass whose sheen was already dimmed with suspicious stains.

"Well," he growled, pointing at Eric, who was staring at him spell-bound with horror and dread, "that seems to be the last of them. Let's finish him off. We want no tell-tales.—Out of the way, you brute." And he lifted his cutlass as though to strike Prince first.

"Hold!" cried Ben, springing forward and grasping Evil-Eye's arm. "Let the boy alone."

"Let him alone," roared Evil-Eye, with a horrible oath. "That I won't. Let go of me, will you?" And wrenching himself free by a tremendous effort, he swung the cutlass high over his head and rushed upon the defenceless boy, who was too terror-stricken to move or cry out.

But quick as Evil-Eye's movements had been, there was another present whose movements were quicker still. With a short, deep growl like a distant roll of thunder, Prince launched himself full at the ruffian's throat. His aim was unerring, and utterly unprepared for so sudden an onset, the man rolled over upon the sand, the cutlass falling harmlessly from his hand.

Content with having brought him to the ground, Prince did not pursue his advantage further, but stood over the prostrate scoundrel, who made no attempt to move, while he implored Ben to drag the dog off him. But this Ben seemed in no hurry to do. He evidently enjoyed his associate's sudden defeat, and felt little sympathy for him in his present predicament. Then as he looked from the growling mastiff to his young master, who had almost forgotten his own fear in his admiration for his faithful dog, a happy thought flashed into his mind. His face brightened, and there was a half-smile upon it, as, turning to Evil-Eye, who scarce dared to breathe lest those great black jaws, so close to his throat, would close tight upon it, he said,—

"Look here, Evil-Eye. I'll take the dog off on one condition. Will you agree?"

"What is that?" groaned Evil-Eye.

"Why, I've taken a fancy to this lad and his dog, and want to keep them for a while, anyway. Now, if you'll promise me that you'll let them alone so long as I want them, I'll get the dog off; but if you won't, I'll just let you have it out with him."

Evil-Eye did not answer at once. Twisting his head, he looked around to see if any other of his companions were near; but there was not a soul in sight, and the storm was still raging.

"All right, Ben, I'll promise," he said sulkily; and then a crafty gleam came into his baleful eye as he added, "And say, Ben, will you give me half your share of this take if I stand by you for the boy? They'll be wanting him finished off, maybe."

Ben was about to say something bitter in reply, but checked himself as though second thoughts were best. Yet he could not entirely conceal his contempt in his tone as he replied,—

"As you like. These two are what I want most this time. But, mind you, Evil-Eye, if any harm comes to either of them through your doing, your own blood shall pay for it, so sure as my name's Ben Harden." Then, turning to Eric, he said,—

"Here, boy, you can call off your dog now."

Eric obeyed the directions at once. "Come here, Prince!" he commanded. "Come to me, sir!"

Prince wagged his tail to indicate that he heard the order, but was evidently in some doubt as to the wisdom of obeying it. According to his way of thinking, the best place for Evil-Eye was just where he had him, and he would like to keep him there a while longer, anyway.

But Eric insisted, and at length the dog obeyed, and came over to him, turning, however, to glance back at Evil-Eye, as though he was just itching to tumble him over again.

Looking very much out of humour, Evil-Eye pulled himself together, and put his hand to his throat in order to make sure that Prince's teeth had done him no injury. Fortunately for him, the high collar of the greatcoat he wore had been turned up all around to keep out the rain, and it had done him still better service by keeping out the mastiff's teeth. So he was really none the worse for the encounter beyond feeling sulky at his discomfiture.

He now for the first time took a good look at Eric, who had also risen to his feet, the excitement of the encounter having made him forget his pain and weakness.

"Humph! rather a likely lad," he grunted. "But he may give us trouble some time. Have you thought of that, Ben?"

"No; but it doesn't matter," answered Ben. "I'll warrant for his not getting us into trouble. We can manage that all right when the time comes."

"Humph! maybe. But it's a risk, all the same," returned Evil-Eye. "But come, we must be off. We've lost too much time already."

The all-prevailing gloom of the day was already deepening into the early dark of late autumn as the three set off across the sands. The spray that the storm tore from the crests of the billows dashed in their faces as they advanced. Eric could not have gone far had not Ben thrown his brawny arm around him, and almost carried him along. Prince trotted quietly at his heels, having quite regained his composure, and resigned himself to the situation.

In this fashion they had gone some distance, and Evil-Eye, who had kept a little ahead, was about to turn off to the right toward the interior of the island, when Prince suddenly sniffed the air eagerly, threw up his head with a curious cry, half whine, half bark, and then bounded away in the direction of the water. Eric stopped to watch him, and following him closely with his eyes, saw that he ran up to a dark object that lay stretched out upon the sand, about fifty yards away. The dog touched it with his nose, and then, lifting his head, gave a long, weird howl, that so startled Eric as to make him forget his weariness. Breaking away from Ben, who, indeed, made no effort to detain him, he hastened over to see what Prince had found.

Darkness was coming on, but before he had got half way to the object he could make out that it was a human body, and a few steps nearer made it plain that the body was that of Major Maunsell.

Horror-stricken, yet hoping that the major might still be living, Eric rushed forward, and throwing himself down beside the motionless form, cried passionately,—

"Major Maunsell! What's the matter? Can't you look up? Oh, surely you're not dead!"

But the major made no response. Beyond all doubt his body was cold in death, and as Eric looked upon the white, set face, he saw that his cries were useless, and that his dear, kind friend had gone from him for ever. He felt as though his heart would break, and glancing around through his tears at the two strange, rough-looking men upon whose mercy the storm had cast him, his own fate seemed so dark and doubtful that he almost wished that, like the major, he too was lying upon the sands in the same quiet sleep.

The discovery of the major's death was a greater shock than the boy, in his exhausted condition, could stand, and when, at the approach of the men, he attempted to rise, faintness overcame him once more, and he fell back unconscious.

When his senses returned, he found himself in a sort of bunk in one corner of a large room containing a number of men, whose forms and faces were made visible by the light from an immense wood-fire that roared and crackled at the farther end of the room. There were at least a score of these men, and, so far as he could make out, they were all rough, shaggy, wild-looking fellows, like Ben and Evil-Eye. The latter he could see plainly, sitting beside a table with a bottle before him, from which he had just taken a deep draught.

The liquor apparently loosened his tongue, for glancing about him with his single eye, whose fitful glare was frightful as the firelight flashed upon it, he began to talk vigorously to those who were sitting near him. At first Eric paid no attention to what he was saying, but when Evil-Eye held up something for the others to admire, he leaned forward curiously to see what it was. There was not sufficient light for him to do this, but Evil-Eye came to his assistance by saying, in an exultant tone,—

"There's a ring for you, my hearties. It'll bring a pot of money, I wager you. And it ought to. I had trouble enough getting it."

"How was that?" inquired a man at his side.

"The thing wouldn't come off—stuck on tight. Had to chop off the finger before I could get it," replied the ruffian, turning the ring over so that the diamond which formed its centre might sparkle to the best advantage for the benefit of his companions, not one of whom but envied him his good luck in getting such a prize.

Eric now saw clearly enough what Evil-Eye was displaying. It was the costly ring which Major Maunsell always wore upon the third finger of his left hand, and whose beauty Eric had many a time admired, for it held a diamond of unusual size and of the purest water, which the major told him had been a sort of heirloom in the Maunsell family for many generations. Eric's blood boiled at the thought of this ring being in such a scoundrel's hands, and of the cruel way in which he had obtained it, and only his utter weakness prevented him from springing at Evil-Eye and snatching the ring out of his hands.

Happily he had not the strength to carry out so rash an impulse, and was forced to content himself with making a solemn resolve to get possession of that ring in some manner, that it might be returned to the major's family. Determination was one of the boy's most marked characteristics. Nothing short of the conviction that it was certainly unattainable could deter him from anything upon which he had once set his heart; and immense as the odds against him in the matter of the ring might be, he vowed with all the vigour of his brave young heart that he would do his utmost to regain his dead friend's precious jewel.

For the present, however, nothing could be done. He was a captive no less than the ring, and, for aught he knew, equally in the power of that brute in human form, who was evidently a leading spirit in the group of ruffians that occupied the room. Clearly enough, his one hope lay in attracting as little attention as possible. He looked anxiously about the room in search of Ben, but could see nothing of him. His good Prince, however, was stretched out upon the floor beside the bunk, sleeping as soundly as though he were in his own cozy quarters at Oakdene. The sight of him comforted Eric not a little. So lonely did he feel that he could not resist the temptation to awake his faithful companion, so he called softly,—

"Prince, Prince, come here!"

At first the mastiff did not hear him, but Eric repeating the call, he awoke, looked up inquiringly, and then, rising slowly to his feet—for he was very tired after the terrible passage through the surf—went over and laid his huge head upon his master's breast.

"Dear old dog!" murmured Eric, fondling him lovingly. "O Prince! what is to become of us? If we were only back in Oakdene again!" And then, as the awful thought rushed in upon his mind that perhaps neither he nor Prince would ever see Oakdene again, or find their way to Dr. Copeland at Halifax, the tears he had been bravely keeping back could no longer be restrained. Sobbing as though his heart would break, he clasped Prince's head tightly in his arms and gave himself up to his grief.

While poor Eric was thus giving way to his feelings, a number of men entered the room, one of them being Ben Harden. He went up to the weeping boy, and sitting down on the edge of the bunk, said in quite a kindly tone,—

"What's the matter, my lad? Feeling homesick, eh? Well, I can't blame you. It's a poor place you've come to. But cheer up, and make the best of it. You'll feel better when you get rested."

With a great effort Eric gulped down his sobs and wiped away his fast-falling tears. He felt much relieved at seeing Ben again, and did his best to give him a smile of welcome as he said,—

"Oh, I'm so glad you've come. Everything seems so strange here."

A grim smile broke the habitual sternness of the big man's face.

"Strange! Yes; no doubt. It is a strange place. Perhaps you'll think it stranger before you leave it," said he—adding in an undertone to himself, so that Eric hardly caught the words, "that is, if you ever do leave it."

A large pot hung on a kind of wooden crane before the fire, and pointing to it Ben asked Eric if he wouldn't like something to eat. Then, without waiting for a reply, he went over to the table, and picking up a plate, proceeded to fill it from the pot, and having added a spoon, brought it back to Eric.

Now, trouble may take away the appetite of older people, but with a hearty, healthy boy hunger may always be trusted to insist upon being attended to. Eric had not tasted food since early morning, and it was now approaching midnight. Could any one who know anything about boys find it in his heart to criticise him if the plateful of savoury stew vanished rapidly before his dexterous wielding of the spoon?

Ben was highly pleased at his *protégé's* vigorous appetite.

"Well done, my hearty!" he exclaimed. "That's the best kind of physic for you. You'll soon be yourself again. Now, then, just you lie down and take a good snooze, and that'll finish the cure."

Eric was just about to throw himself back upon the pillow when he caught sight of Prince, who had been watching him with eager eyes while he satisfied his hunger.

"My poor Prince!" he cried. "I was forgetting all about you.—Please, can't he have some dinner too?"

"Sartin!" said Ben. "The brute must be hungry. I'll give him a good square meal." And filling a tin dish from the pot, he set it before the mastiff, who attacked it ravenously.

Eric felt decidedly better for his hearty meal. A luxurious sense of warmth and languor stole over him. He stretched himself out upon his comfortable couch, and in a few moments sank into a deep, dreamless sleep. Prince having licked the dish until it shone again, resumed his position beside the bunk, and fell asleep also.

CHAPTER V.

ERIC LOOKS ABOUT HIM.

It was broad daylight when the boy awoke, and he felt very well pleased at finding no one in the room but Ben, who sat by the table, evidently waiting for him to open his eyes. As soon as he did so the latter noticed it, and coming up to the bunk, said in his gruff way,—

"Oh, ho! Awake at last. Was wondering if you were going to sleep all day. Feel like turning out?"

"Of course," replied Eric, brightly. "I feel all right now."

On getting out of the bunk, however, he found himself so dreadfully stiff and sore that it was positively painful to move, and he had much difficulty in dragging himself over to the table, where he found a pile of ship's biscuit and a pannikin of tea awaiting him. He did not feel at all so hungry as he had the night before, and this very plain repast seemed very unattractive, accustomed as he was to the best of fare. He nibbled at the biscuit, took a sip of the tea, and then pushed the things away, saying,—

"I don't want any breakfast, thank you. I'm not a bit hungry."

Ben was too shrewd not to guess the true reason of the boy's indifferent appetite.

"There's not much choice of grub on Sable Island," said he, with one of his grim smiles. "You'll have to take kindly to hard-tack and tea if you don't want to starve."

"But really I am not hungry," explained Eric eagerly, afraid of seeming not to appreciate his friend's hospitality. "If I were, I'd eat the biscuits fast enough, for I'm quite fond of them."

Ben now proceeded to fill and light a big pipe.

"Do you smoke?" he asked, after he had got it in full blast.

"Oh, no," answered Eric. "My father doesn't believe in boys smoking, and has forbidden me to learn."

"Your father's a sensible man, my boy," said Ben; then added, "Well, you'd best stay about the hut to-day, since you feel so stiff. I've got to go off, but I'll be back by mid-day." He put on his hat and went away, leaving Eric and Prince in possession of the establishment.

Eric did not by any means like the idea of being left alone, but he naturally shrank from saying so. He went to the door and regretfully looked after the tall figure striding swiftly over the sand until it disappeared behind a hillock, beyond which he thought must be the ocean.

Now that he was left entirely to his own resources, Eric's curiosity began to assert itself. Had he but known in what direction to go, and felt equal to the task, his first business would certainly have been to set forth in search of the scene of the wreck, if haply he might find traces of other survivors besides himself.

But neither could he tell where to go, nor was he fit to walk any great distance. For aught he knew, he might be miles from the beach where the*Francis* finally struck. Anyway, Evil-Eye was certain to be there, hunting for more prizes, and he had no wish to encounter him. So he proceeded to examine his strange surroundings.

The hut—for, despite its size, it was really nothing more than a hut—was a very curious building. It had evidently been put together by many hands, out of the wreckage of many ships, the builders apparently being more proficient in ship-carpentry than in house-joinery. Their labours had resulted, through an amazing adaptation of knees, planking, stanchions, and bulk-heads, in a long, low-ceilinged, but roomy building, something after the shape of a large vessel's poop. For lighting and ventilation it depended upon a number of port-holes irregularly put in. Running around two sides of the room was a row of bunks, very much like those in a forecastle, the tier being two high. Eric counted them. There were just thirty, and he wondered if each had an occupant. If so, he must have slept in Ben's last night, and where, then, had Ben himself slept?

Upon the walls of the other two sides of the room hung a great number of weapons of various kinds—cutlasses, swords, muskets, dirks, daggers, and pistols, a perfect armoury, all carefully burnished and ready for use. They strongly excited Eric's curiosity, and he occupied himself examining them one by one. One pair of pistols especially attracted his attention. They were of the very latest make, and the handles were beautifully inlaid with silver. He took one from the wall, and aimed at one of the port-holes with it. As he did so a thought flashed into his mind that gave him an electric thrill, and sent the blood bounding wildly through his veins.

What if that port-hole were the repulsive countenance of Evil-Eye, and they were alone together? Would he be able to resist the impulse to give with his forefinger the slight pressure upon the finely-balanced trigger that would send a bullet crashing into the ruffian's brain? So intense was his excitement that he almost staggered under its influence. For the first time in his life an overmastering passion for revenge, for retribution, took possession of him, and carried him out of himself. Smooth, clear, and bright as the lovely stream that watered the Oakdene meadows had been the current of his life hitherto. To few boys had the lines fallen in pleasanter places. Yet this happy fortune had not rendered him unmanly or irresolute. He was capable of conceiving and carrying out any purpose that lay within the range of a boy's powers. The Copeland courage and the Copeland determination were his inheritance.

Now never before had he been brought into contact with any one who had so roused his repulsion or hatred as Evil-Eye. Not only because of his hideous appearance and threatened violence, but because of Ben's dark hints and his own suspicions as to Evil-Eye being no better than a murderer, the very depths of his nature were stirred, and he felt as though it would be but right to inflict summary vengeance at the first opportunity.

Trembling with these strange, wild thoughts, he held the pistol still pointed at the port-hole, and unconsciously pressing upon the trigger, there was a sharp report, which caused Prince, dozing comfortably by the fire, to spring to his feet with a startled growl, following the crash of broken glass, as the bullet pierced the port-lid.

Almost at the same moment the door was thrown roughly open and Evil-Eye entered the room.

"What are you doing with my pistols?" he cried, his face aflame with rage, as he strode toward Eric.

Scarce knowing what he was doing, Eric snatched up the other pistol and darted around the big table, so that it would form a barrier between himself and Evil-Eye. His hand was perfectly steady now, and levelling the pistol at his assailant, he said in a firm tone,—-

"Let me alone, or I'll shoot you."

With a fearful oath the ruffian drew a pistol from his belt, and in another moment blood would undoubtedly have been shed, had not Ben Harden rushed in through the open door, and snatching Evil-Eye's pistol out of his hand, thrown it to the other end of the room, where it went off without harm to any one.

"You scoundrel!" he roared. "If you don't leave that boy alone, I will break every bone in your body."

At first Evil-Eye was so completely taken aback by this unexpected interference that he seemed dazed for a moment. Then his hand went again to his belt, as though he would turn his baffled fury upon Ben. But evidently a wiser second thought prevailed, and choking down his wrath, he growled out contemptuously,—

"Don't be in such a stew. I'm not going to hurt your baby. I was only teaching him manners, and not to meddle with other people's belongings without first asking their leave."

This speech drew Ben's attention to the pistol Eric still held in his hand.

"Ah," said he, "you've got one of Evil-Eye's pets there, have you? Well, put it back in its place, and don't touch it again."

Feeling very confused, Eric replaced the pistols carefully, their owner watching him with a malign glare which boded him no good. Its meaning was not lost upon observant Ben.

"Come, my lad," said he; "a bit of an airing will do you good. Put on your cap, and come out with me."

Only too glad to obey, Eric picked up his cap, and calling to Prince, followed Ben out into the open air, leaving Evil-Eye alone in the hut.

The sun was shining brightly, the sky was almost cloudless, and the wind blew as softly and innocently from the south as though it had not raged with fatal fury but a few hours before. Eric's spirits, which had been wofully depressed by the events of the past two days, began to rise a little, and he looked about him with much interest as he trudged along through the deep sand.

Ben appeared to be in no mood for talking, and stalked on ahead in moody silence, puffing hard at the short black pipe which was hardly ever away from his mouth except at meal-time and when he was sleeping. Eric therefore did not bother him with questions, and found companionship in Prince, who showed lively satisfaction in being out-of-doors, frisking about and barking loudly in the exuberance of his glee. One good night's rest and plenty to eat had been sufficient to completely restore his strength. He looked and felt quite equal to anything that might be required of him, and was an inexpressible comfort to Eric, to whom he seemed much more than a mere dog—a protector and friend, who could be trusted to the uttermost.

Half-an-hour's walking brought Ben to the highest point of a sand-ridge, where he threw himself, waiting for Eric, who had lagged behind a little, to come up.

"Sit ye down, lad," said he, when the boy reached him. "You're feeling tired, no doubt."

Eric was tired, and very glad indeed to seat himself near Ben, who continued to puff away at his pipe, as though he had nothing more to say. Thus left to himself, Eric let his eyes wander over the strange and striking scene spread out before him.

He was upon the crest of a sand-hill, a hundred feet or more in height, which sloped to the beach, upon whose glistening sands the great billows were breaking, although the day was clear and calm. Far out beyond the serried lines of white-maned sea-coursers the ocean could be seen sleeping peacefully. Here and there, upon the sand-bars, the hulls of vessels in various stages of destruction told plainly how common was the fate which had befallen the *Francis*, and how rich a field the wreckers had chosen for their dreadful business.

Turning to his right, Eric saw a long narrow lake in the middle of the island, its banks densely grown with rushes and lilies. Upon its placid surface flocks of ducks were paddling, while snipes and sand-pipers hopped along the margin. The valley of the lake presented a curious contrast to those portions of the island that faced seaward, for it was thickly carpeted with coarse grass and wild vines, which were still green enough to be grateful to the eye weary of the monotony of sand and sea.

Upon the left the island rose and fell, a succession of sand-hills. Far in the distance, a faint line of white showed where it once more touched the ocean, and gave cause for other lines of roaring surges. All this and more had Eric time to take in before Ben broke silence. He had been regarding him very thoughtfully for a few moments, and at length he spoke,—

"Well, lad," said he, "I've been thinking much about ye. I've saved your life, but I'm not so clear in my mind but what it 'ud have been best to have let you go with the others."

Eric gave a start of surprise, and there was an alarmed tone in his voice, as he exclaimed,—

"Why, Mr. Ben, what makes you say that?"

"Well, you see, it's just this way," answered Ben slowly, as though he were puzzling out the best way to state the case. "You're in a mighty bad box, and no mistake. Evil-Eye does not fancy you, and will take the first chance to do for you, if he can keep his own skin whole. Dead men tell no tales is what he goes by; and if the folks over there"—jerking his thumb in the direction of the mainland—"only knew what goes on here, they'd be pretty sure to want to put a stop to it, and make us all smart for it finely. Now, it's not likely you want to join us; and I'm no less sure that Evil-Eye will take precious good care not to let you go, for fear you should get his neck into the noose. That's the only thing he's afraid of. And so it just bothers me to make out what's to be the end of the business."

CHAPTER VI.

BEN HARDEN.

As the words fell one by one from Ben's lips, Eric realized more and more clearly how critical was his situation. In his gladness at escape from the present peril of the wreck, he had forgotten to take thought for the future; but now he was brought face to face with a state of affairs by which that future was filled with dark foreboding. Little as he had seen of the men into whose midst he had been so strangely thrown, it was enough to make very plain to him that they wanted no witness of their doings.

So far they had been too much occupied with their own concerns to take much notice of him; but once he became the object of their attention, the question as to his disposal must be settled. The issue was more than doubtful, to say the least.

An awful feeling of desolation and despair came upon him. He seemed unable to utter a word, but looked up into Ben's bronzed face with an expression in which pathetic appeal was so mingled with harrowing dread as to touch this strange man.

He sprang to his feet, dashed his pipe out of his mouth, clenched his huge fists, and shouted aloud, as though all the other wreckers were there to hear,—

"They had better take care! I saved ye, and I'm going to stand by ye. Whoever wants to do you harm'll have to reckon with Ben Harden first; and come what may, I'll get you off this place with a whole skin, somehow."

Eric was as much surprised at Ben's sudden display of strong feeling as he had been alarmed by his ominous words. He gazed at him, with wide-open mouth, until the wrecker, recovering his self-control by an evident effort, threw himself down on the sand again, picked up his pipe, carefully relit it, and vigorously resumed puffing forth clouds of smoke.

It was some time before he spoke again. In a quiet, natural tone he asked Eric,—

"Have you any notion, my lad, why I troubled myself about ye at all?"

Eric shook his head, and there was something inexpressibly winning in his smile as he answered,—

"No, sir. Unless because you have too kind a heart to let Evil-Eye do me any harm."

Ben smiled in return, but it was in a grim sort of a way.

"My heart was softer once than it is now. There were better days then, and never did I think that I'd come to be a wrecker on Sable Island," said he; and the remembrance of those better days evidently gave him saddening thoughts, for he relapsed into the moody silence that was his wont. It continued so long that Eric began to feel uncomfortable, and was about to move away a little, in order to have a frolic with Prince, when Ben roused himself, and motioned him to draw near him.

"Sit ye down in front of me, my lad," said he, "and listen to me a bit, and I'll tell you why I couldn't find it in my heart to let any harm come to you. I had a boy of my own once, as trim a lad as ever sat in a boat; and many a fine trip we made together, for I was at an honest trade then, and wasn't ashamed to take my boy into it. Ah, lad! those were the good times. We went fishing on the Banks, getting our outfit at Halifax, and selling our fare there. But our home was at Chester, where I had a snug cottage, all my own, without a shilling of debt on it, and pretty well fitted up too. The wife—she was the best wife that ever I knew—she looked after the cottage, and we looked after the little schooner; and after each trip we'd stay at home awhile and have a little time together.

"We were mostly always in luck on the Banks, and it was not often the *Sea-Slipper* missed a good fare, if there were any fish to be caught. And so it went on, until I lost my lad. He and his mate were out in their dory fishing, and the cod were plentiful, and they were so full of catching them that they did not notice the fog coming up and creeping all around them. They lost their bearings, and no man ever set eyes on them again.

"I didn't give up hoping I'd find them for months afterwards. I cruised about the Banks, I called at all the ports that sent out Bankers, and I tried at Halifax, Boston, New York, and other big places, hoping that some ship might have picked them up. But not a word did I hear. There was a heavy blow right after the fog, and no doubt they were lost in that. I lost a lot of time hunting for my boy, and it seemed as though when he went my luck followed him. Everything went wrong. The fish would hardly touch my hooks, and I never got a full fare. Then the wife died. She never held up her head after the day I came home without our boy. I took to the drink. It didn't make matters any better, of course, but I couldn't keep from it.

"I got knocking about with a bad lot of chaps; and the end of it was, some of us came here. I don't care how soon it's all over with me. I hate this business, and I hate myself."

Here Ben came to a pause, as though he had said more than he intended; and Eric, not knowing what to interpose, looked at him in silent sympathy, until he began again.

"But I haven't told ye why I saved ye from Evil-Eye.

"Well, it was just this way. When I found ye, you were lying on the sand like as though you were asleep; and you fairly gave me a start, you looked so like my own boy. He was just about your age when he was lost, and you'd be much the same size, and he had brown hair just like yours.

"If my boy had been lying half-dead on the beach, I'd have thought any man worse than a brute that wouldn't help the lad. So I just made up my mind to take your part, Evil-Eye or no Evil-Eye; and now I'm going to stick to it."

Having spoken thus, Ben put his pipe back between his lips, evidently having no more to say. Eric hardly knew how to give expression to his feelings. Sympathy for his rescuer's troubles and gratitude for his assurance of safe-keeping filled his heart. The tears gathered in his eyes, and his voice trembled as, turning to the big man beside him, he laid his hand upon his knee, and looking up into his face, said,—

"You've been very good to me, Mr. Ben. You're the only friend I've got here except Prince, and I'm sure you won't let any harm come to me, if you can help it. And I'm so sorry about your son. You see, we've both lost somebody: you've lost your boy, and I—I've lost my mother."

His voice sank to a whisper as he uttered the words, and the tears he had been bravely keeping back overflowed upon his cheeks.

Ben said not a word. There was a suspicious glistening about his eyelids, and the quite superfluous vigour of his puffing told plainly enough that he was deeply moved. After a moment he rose to his feet, knocked the ashes out of his pipe, and putting it into his pocket, said,—

"Come, lad, let us go back to the hut."

The two retraced their steps to the wreckers' abode. Eric now felt more at ease than he had since the shipwreck. With such protectors as Ben and Prince he surely had not much to fear, even in the evil company among which he had been cast. As to the future—well, it certainly did seem dark. But he had been taught to put trust in the Heavenly Father to whom he prayed, and he looked up to him now for help and guidance.

When they arrived at the hut they found the whole party of wreckers there, waiting somewhat impatiently for a huge negro to serve them their supper.

This negro did duty as cook; they called him Black Joe. They took little notice of the new-comers, and Eric, going quietly over to his bunk, sat down on the edge and looked about him. This was his first opportunity of getting a good look at his strange companions.

By listening to their conversation and studying their countenances he made out that the majority of them were English, but that there were a few Frenchmen amongst them. There was only one negro, a stalwart, bull-necked, bullet-headed fellow, with a good-natured face, who seemed the butt of the others, and a target for their oaths and jeers, as he bustled about the fireplace preparing their food.

The whole party appeared to be in excellent humour, the cause thereof being plainly enough the fact of the *Francis* having proved so rich a prize. Each man had been able to secure sufficient plunder to satisfy him, so there was no necessity for quarrelling over the division. They each had some precious find to boast of, and they vied with one another in relating with great gusto their successful efforts after the wreckage. From what they said, Eric gathered that the *Francis* did not break up after striking. Her stout oak frame resisted the fiercest attempts of the billows to tear it asunder. The storm subsided during the night, and the men were able in the morning to make their way to the wreck, and despoil her of whatever took their fancy.

The thousands of valuable books, and the holdful of costly but cumbrous furniture, they contemptuously left to the mercy of wind and wave. The great store of gold and silver plate, the casks of finest wines, the barrels and cases of delicious biscuits, conserves, pickles, and other dainties, together with the racks of muskets, swords, and other weapons—these were all very much to their liking. Moreover, the clothing chests had been ransacked, each man helping himself according to his fancy. The result was a display of gorgeous uniforms and elegant apparel that would have been quite imposing had not the faces and manners of the wearers been so ludicrously out of keeping with their costumes.

Little did Prince Edward imagine, when ordering liberal additions to his wardrobe, that those resplendent garments were destined to be worn to tatters on the backs of the wreckers of Sable Island. What would have been his feelings could he have seen Evil-Eye strutting about as proud as a turkey-cock in the superb uniform intended for the commander of the forces at Halifax?

Although the profuse profanity of the speakers shocked and sickened him, Eric listened attentively to all that was said, in the hope of picking up something about his future. But the wreckers were too much occupied with their own affairs to pay any attention to him. Presently Black Joe announced that supper was ready, whereupon they all stopped talking, and fell to with ravenous appetites.

The table looked curiously out of keeping with its associations of squalid hut and coarse, brutal men. It was covered with a cloth of richest damask that should have adorned a royal dining-room, and set out with china, glass, plate, and cutlery of corresponding elegance. It filled Eric with indignation and disgust to see the wreckers hacking their meat with ivory-handled knives, impaling their potatoes upon silver forks, and quenching their thirst by copious draughts out of cut-glass goblets, which seemed to be desecrated by their foul touch.

Ben motioned him to a seat beside himself, and helped him bountifully. Ill at ease as the boy felt, he was very hungry, and was glad to do full justice to the coarse but plentiful fare provided by Black Joe. The wine he would not touch.

The hearty supper and the abundant wine put the men in even better humour than before, and Ben now saw his opportunity to carry out a plan that had been forming in his mind. Rising to his feet, he secured his companions' attention by rapping loudly upon the table with the handle of his knife, and then proceeded to surprise them by making a little speech; for so chary of his words was he, as a usual thing, that they sometimes called him Silent Ben.

"I want a word with you, mates," said he; and at once every face was turned toward him.

"You see this boy here. Now, I've taken a great liking to him, and I'm willing that he and his dog shall be counted as part of my share of this last prize. That's all right, ain't it?"

"Ay, ay, Ben; right enough," came from half-a-dozen of them, while some of the others looked a little doubtful, as if they didn't know exactly what was coming.

CHAPTER VII.

A SABLE ISLAND WINTER.

"Well now, look here, mates," Ben continued; "fair and square's the word between us, ain't it? If I choose to take a notion to these two here, it's my own lookout, and it's not for any other chap to be interfering with me, any more than I'd be after wanting your things, eh?"

They were beginning to see what he was driving at now, and one of them said, with a sort of sneer,—

"You're not afraid of any one wanting your boy, or his dog either, are you?"

"Not exactly," answered Ben; "but what I've on my mind is this: seeing they're my property, I don't want any one to meddle with them or give them any trouble—that's only fair, ain't it?"

"Fair enough, Ben; but what are you going to do with the boy when we leave here?" asked one. And there was a murmur of assent to the question.

"That'll be all right, mates," replied Ben promptly. "I'll be surety that he doesn't get us into any trouble. You just leave that to me, and I'll warrant you I'll get him away from us quiet enough. What do you say, mates?"

Although by dint of bluster and brutality Evil-Eye had forced his way to a sort of leadership among the wreckers, there was really none of them with so much influence as Ben. With the exception of Evil-Eye they were all now quite ready to accept his assurances of Eric not proving a source of trouble, and to consent to his remaining with them. Evil-Eye growled and grumbled a good deal, but could get nobody to heed him; and Ben, satisfied that he had carried his point, and that Eric and Prince were safe, took his seat again, and lit his pipe for a good smoke. He was perfectly sincere in promising that Eric would not get his associates into any trouble. He certainly never imagined what would be the result of his taking him under his protection. Could he have had a peep into the future, perhaps he would have hesitated before becoming his champion. As it was, he gave himself no concern upon the point.

Eric felt wonderfully relieved at the result of his protector's appeal. It settled his position among his strange, uncongenial companions. They might take no notice of him if they chose—indeed, that was just what he would prefer—but they had, at all events, not only recognized but consented to his presence, and this took a great load off his mind.

Although his objections had been ignored by his companions, Evil-Eye was by no means disposed to give up altogether his designs upon Eric. There were two reasons why he hungered for the boy's life. It was against his principle of dead men telling no tales that he should be spared; and, again, he hated Ben, and the mere fact of his being interested in Eric was quite sufficient to cause the innocent lad to get a share of that hatred.

In the days that followed, Eric could not fail to be conscious of the frequency with which the ruffian's one eye was turned upon him, and of the hyena-like look with which it regarded him. Happy for him was it that there was a restraining influence which kept that awful look from finding its way into fitting deed.

Though they did not distinctly recognize any leader—their motto being each man for himself, and one as good as another—the wreckers regarded Ben with a respect accorded no other member of the motley crew. This was in part due to his great size and strength, and in part to his taciturn, self-contained ways, which prevented any of that familiarity that so quickly breeds contempt.

Evil-Eye feared Ben no less than he hated him, and dared not openly attempt anything against him, although the fire of his fury burned hotly within his breast. In this fear of Ben, much more than in the decision of the other wreckers, lay Eric's safety. Ere long, this defence was strengthened in a manner most strange, startling, and happily most effective.

A week of almost incessant stormy weather had compelled the wreckers to spend most of their time in the hut. Finding the hours hang heavy on their hands, many of them had sought solace in drink, of which the *Francis's* fine stock of wines and liquors furnished an unstinted supply. No one drank more deeply than Evil-Eye. Day after day was passed in a state alternating between coarse hilarity and maudlin stupor; Ben, on the other hand, hardly touched the liquor, contenting himself with sipping a little at his meals. It was well, indeed, that he should be so moderate, for his cool head and strong hand were in demand more than once to prevent serious conflicts among his intoxicated companions.

Eric, in spite of the stormy weather, kept as much out of doors as possible. He preferred the buffeting of the wintry winds to the close atmosphere of the hut, foul with oaths, and reeking with tobacco and spirits.

Evil-Eye's carouse had continued several days. Early one night, after he had fallen into a sottish sleep upon his bunk, and the others had, later on, one by one turned in for the night, leaving the room in a silence broken only by the heavy breathing and stertorous snoring of the sleepers, the whole hut was suddenly aroused by an appalling yell from Evil-Eye. Starting up, his companions saw him, by the light of a moonbeam that strayed in through one of the portholes, rise to his feet with an expression of the most frantic terror upon his hideous countenance, as he shrieked at the top of his voice,—

"I will—I swear I will—if you'll only let me alone!"

Then, throwing up his arms, he fell over, foaming, in a fit.

For some minutes the hut was a scene of wild confusion as its bewildered inmates, so suddenly aroused from their sleep, stumbled about in the darkness trying to find out what was the matter. But Ben, who was not easily frightened, soon restored order by striking a light, and showing that whatever may have been the matter with Evil-Eye, there was certainly no real cause for alarm. Thereupon, with many a growl at him for disturbing their night's rest, most of them grumblingly went back to sleep.

A few thought it worth while to see what was the matter with Evil-Eye, and of these Ben took command. Little as he loved the ruffian, he could not find it in his heart to let him die for lack of a little care. So, under his direction, the struggling man was lifted out upon the floor. His face was splashed with water, while his arms and legs were chafed by rough hands. In a little while the patient's struggles grew less violent, the purple hue left his face, and his breathing became more natural. Presently, with a great sigh, he fell into a heavy sleep, from which he did not awake for many hours.

Although pestered with questions upon his return to consciousness as to the cause of his strange behaviour, he refused to give any reason. But there were two changes in him too noticeable not to excite the remark of his associates—he was much more moderate in the use of wine, taking care not to drink to excess; and his attitude toward Eric became curiously different. Instead of regarding him with his former look of hungering hatred, he now seemed to have a feeling of dread. He shrank from being near him, avoiding him in every possible way; treating him, in fact, much as a dog would a man who had been especially cruel to him.

Ben and Eric at once noted the change, and were well pleased at it. Some time after, they learned the cause. It seemed that the evening Evil-Eye had acted so strangely he had been awakened from his drunken sleep about midnight by a startling vision.

It was the form of a tall man in a military uniform dripping with sea-water and soiled with sand. On his face was the pallor of death, and his eyes had an awful, far-away expression, as though they were looking through the startled sleeper. Fixing them steadfastly upon Evil-Eye, whose blood seemed to freeze in his veins, he held up his forefinger as if commanding attention, and pointed to the bunk where Eric lay sleeping. At the same time his face took on a threatening look, and his lips moved.

Although no words reached Evil-Eye's ears, he understood. As the spectre stood before him, so intense was his terror that it broke the spell which locked his lips, and he shrieked out the words already mentioned. He knew no more until, at broad daylight, he found himself weak and miserable in his berth.

Like many men of his kind, Evil-Eye was very superstitious. After the vision he looked upon Eric as being under the protection of some ghostly being that would for ever haunt any one who did him any harm. Henceforth Eric had nothing to fear from him.

Winter on Sable Island is not like winter on the mainland. The Gulf Stream prevents any long continuance of cold. The snow comes in violent storms, and fills the valleys with drifts; but these soon vanish. There is more rain and fog than snow, even in mid-winter; and the herds of wild, shaggy, sharp-boned ponies which scamper from end to end of the island have no difficulty in finding plenty to eat among the grasses which grow rankly in every sheltered spot.

These ponies were a great source of amusement to Eric. But for them and the rabbits, which were even more numerous, the winter, wearisome at best, would have been simply intolerable.

The wreckers had captured a score of the ponies, and broken them in after a fashion. They were kept near the hut, in a large corral built of driftwood, and there were plenty of saddles and bridles.

Now if there was one manly accomplishment more than another upon which Eric prided himself it was his horsemanship. He had been put upon a pony when only five years old, and had been an enthusiastic rider ever since. At Oakdene he had ridden to hounds since he was twice five years of age, and there was not a lad in the county with a firmer seat in the saddle or a more masterful touch of the reins. The saddles and bridles at Sable Island were poor things compared with those he had been accustomed to; and the ponies themselves were about as wicked and vicious as animals of that size could be. But this only lent an additional zest to the amusement of riding them. Their bad behaviour did not daunt Eric in the least. With Ben's assistance a pony would be caught in the corral and saddled, and then off he would go for a long, lively gallop, Prince, as full of glee as himself, barking and bounding along at his side.

Very often Ben would keep him company, for there was an old black stallion of unusual size which seemed equal to the task of bearing his huge frame. Then Eric's happiness was complete, for every day he was growing fonder of the big man who had saved him from a dreadful death, and who now treated him with paternal tenderness.

With the keen wintry air making his cheeks tingle, he would scamper off at full speed for mile after mile, while Ben lumbered along more slowly, thoroughly enjoying the boy's vigour and daring. Then, halting until Ben overtook him, he would canter on quietly.

An amusement of which Eric never tired was chasing the wild ponies, as though he wanted to catch one of them. Climbing one of the sand-hills, he would look about until he sighted a herd grazing quietly in the hollows, and guarded as usual by a touzle-maned stallion of mature years. Making a wide detour, and carefully concealing his approach by keeping the hillocks between himself and the ponies, he would get as near as he possibly could without being seen. If necessary, he dismounted and crept along on his hands and knees, dragging his own pony by the bridle, while Prince followed.

When concealment was no longer possible, he would spring into his saddle, and with wild shouts charge down upon the startled ponies; and they would gallop off in headlong stampede.

One afternoon, while thus amusing himself, he had quite an exciting experience, and rather a narrow escape from injury. He had stampeded a herd of ponies, and picking out a sturdy little youngster as his particular prey, was pressing him pretty closely, when the pony charged straight up the side of a hill. As it was not steep, Eric followed hard after him, taking for granted the slope would be about the same on the other side. Instead of that, the hill fell away abruptly. Over plunged the hunted pony. Unable to check his own animal, full of the spirit of the chase, over plunged Eric too. For a moment both ponies kept their feet; but the treacherous sand giving way beneath them, they rolled head over heels. Eric happily got free from his horse in time to save himself from being crushed underneath it; but when they all reached the bottom in a heap together, he could not escape the frantically pawing hoofs, and one of them struck him such a blow upon the head as to stun him.

When he recovered he found himself lying upon the sand, not a pony in sight, and Prince licking his face with affectionate anxiety. His head ached sharply, and he felt somewhat sore after his tremendous tumble; but not a bone was broken nor a joint sprained. Thankful at having gotten off so well, he made the best of his way back to the hut.

Ben was greatly pleased at the adventure, and regretted he had not been there when ponies, boy, and dog rolled down the hill together.

"You ought to let your friends know when you're going to give a performance like that, my lad," said he, after a hearty laugh. "It's too good to keep to yourself."

"Perhaps you'd like me to repeat it for you," Eric suggested.

"No indeed, Eric. You got off all right that time, but you might break your precious neck the next. How would you like to have a try at a morse? The men tell me they saw a lot of them at the west end this morning; and as you're so fond of hunting, there's something well worth killing."

CHAPTER VIII

ANXIOUS TIMES.

"How would I like it?" cried Eric, his face beaming. "Why, above all things. I've often seen pictures of the great ugly creatures, and I think it would be just splendid to shoot one and get his tusks."

"All right, my boy," replied Ben. "We'll start the first thing in the morning."

Accordingly, the next morning the two set out upon their ponies for the west end. Ben carried a heavy musket that would send a load of slugs through a ship's side, and Eric a light smooth-bore, the accuracy of which he had proved by frequent practice. As they would be away all day, they took plenty of biscuits with them. Prince, of course, accompanied them, and as soon as they had disposed of breakfast they started.

There were many creatures to be found on Sable Island in those days which would be vainly sought for now. Besides the ponies, a large number of wild cattle and hogs roamed about the interior, and furnished the wreckers with abundant meat; while during the winter the morse, or walrus, and the great Greenland seal paid the beaches regular visits. The common harbour seal was there all the year round. Of these animals, only the ponies and common seals still remain; the others have been all killed off.

When Ben and Eric drew near the end of the island they dismounted and tethered the ponies, so that they could not run back to the corral. They then made their way cautiously to the edge of the bank thrown up by the waves. Ben was a little ahead of Eric, and the moment he peeped over the bank he turned and motioned Eric to follow.

"Look, lad!" said he, in a voice full of excitement, as he pointed to the beach in front. "There they are! Aren't they beauties?"

Eric looked, and his face showed the surprise he had too much sense to put into words. "Beauties!" he thought to himself. "Why, they are the most hideous monsters I ever saw in my life."

And they certainly were hideous, with their huge, dun-coloured, ungainly bodies, their bullet heads, their grizzly beards, their terrible tusks, and their bulging eyes. They looked as ugly as some nightmare vision. Plucky as he was,

Eric could not restrain a tremor as he gazed at them. But he had no time to indulge his feelings, for Ben said in a hoarse whisper,—

"You take that tusker right in front of you, and I'll take the big fellow to the right, and when I say 'Fire!' let drive. Be sure and aim right at the nose."

Eric's heart was beating wildly, and he could scarcely breathe for excitement; but his hand was steady as he drew the musket to his shoulder, and took careful aim at the nose of the walrus Ben had assigned to him. Giving a quick glance to see that all was ready, Ben called "Fire!"

Like the report of one the two muskets cracked together, and the marksmen peered eagerly through the smoke to see the result. Clearly enough their aim had been good; for while the remainder of the little pack of walruses lumbered off into the water snorting with terror, the two that had been picked out as targets did not follow. Ben's fell over on the sand, to all appearance dead; but Eric's plunged madly about, seeming to be too bewildered to take refuge in flight.

Hastily reloading, the hunters rushed upon their prey, and Ben, seizing a good opportunity, put another charge of slugs into the struggling creature's head, just behind the ear, which cut short its sufferings.

"Hurrah!" cried Ben, radiant with pride and satisfaction. "We've got them both, and no mistake. We'll each have a fine pair of tusks, won't we?"

Eric was no less delighted, and all his nervousness having vanished, executed a sort of war-dance around the prostrate forms of the sea-monsters, which looked all the uglier the closer he got to them. Drawing a big knife from his belt, Ben approached his walrus to sever the head from the body, Eric standing a little distance off to watch him. They were quite sure the creature was dead; but the instant the sharp steel touched its neck it came to life, for it had been only stunned. With a sudden sweep of its fore-flipper, it hurled Ben over upon his back, sending the knife flying from his hand.

"Eric! quick! for God's sake!" cried Ben, as he fell.

The infuriated monster was right over him. In another moment those terrible tusks would have been buried in his body, when, with a roar like that of a lion, Prince launched himself full at the walrus's head, and his great fangs closed tightly in the soft part where the head joins the neck. Uttering a roar quite equal to the dog's, the morse turned upon his new assailant; but just as he did so, Eric's rifle spoke again. Its bullet crashed into the monster's brain, and with a mad flurry, which loosened even Prince's hold, it rolled over upon the sand, this time dead beyond question.

Ben sprang to his feet, and rushing upon Eric flung his arms around him, and gave him a hug that fairly squeezed the breath out of him. Then, without a word, he turned to Prince, and repeated the operation. He then expressed his gratitude in these words,—

"It was a good day for me when I saved your lives. You've done me good ever since; and now you've saved my life, and it's only tit for tat. All right, my lad; so long as there's a drop of blood in my body, no harm shall come to either of you that Ben Harden can fend off."

The business of beheading, which had been so startlingly interrupted, was now resumed. From the way Ben handled his knife, he was evidently quite experienced at the work. They wanted only the tusks, but to get them out in perfect condition, it would be necessary to boil the heads until the flesh came off readily; so they had to take them back to the hut for that purpose.

Well satisfied with the result of their hunt, they ate their lunch and took a good rest before returning to the hut, which they reached early in the afternoon. They both felt that they were now bound to each other by ties of peculiar strength. Eric, uncertain and full of difficulty as to the future, somehow felt convinced that Ben would bring it out all right for him. He little imagined how much he would help himself in escaping.

Chasing ponies and hunting walruses were not the only amusements Sable Island afforded Eric. As has been already mentioned, the grassy dells abounded with rabbits and the marshy lake and ponds with wild fowl. The rabbit-shooting was really capital sport. The bunnies were fine big fellows, as lively and wary as any sportsman could wish, and to secure a good bag of them meant plenty of hard work.

It was the rabbit-hunting that found Prince in his glory. Had he been a greyhound instead of a mastiff he could not have entered more heartily into the chase. To be sure, he proved, upon the whole, rather more of a hindrance than a help; but no suspicion of this fact ever dashed his bright spirit, and not for the world would Eric have hinted it to him. His redeeming quality lay in his retrieving, for he had been carefully trained to fetch and carry, and he quickly learned to hunt out and bring to them the victims of their muskets. The rabbits were not killed in the mere wantonness of sport. There was always an active demand for them at the hut, where Black Joe made them into savoury stews.

About the same time as the walruses came great numbers of the Greenland seal, which a little later brought forth their funny little whelps. These looked like amphibious puppies as they sprawled about the beach or scuttled off into the water. They took Eric's boyish fancy so strongly that he longed to have one for a pet.

Ben soon gratified him by creeping cautiously upon the pack one day, and grasping by the tail a fine, sleek, shiny little fellow. After a couple of weeks' confinement in a pen, that Eric built for him, with constant, kind attention, the captive became so contented with his new life, and so attached to his young master, that he was allowed his liberty. He showed not the slightest disposition to run away. Eric found him quite as intelligent and docile as a dog, and taught him many amusing tricks.

So long as the weather was fine Eric had plenty of cures for low spirits. But in the winter the proportion of fine days to foul is very small on Sable Island. For a whole week at a time the sun would not appear, and long storms were frequent. Happily, there was one resource at hand for the stormy weather.

Among the spoils of the *Francis* was a leather-covered box, so handsome and so heavy that one of the wreckers, feeling sure it contained something valuable, brought it carefully ashore. When he broke it open he was much disgusted to find that it contained nothing but books. He flung it into a corner, boasting that "he had no book larnin', and what's more, didn't want none."

Eric afterwards picked it up, and was delighted to find in it a large assortment of interesting books. He stowed the box carefully away at the back of his bunk, and thenceforth, when compelled to stay indoors, was never without a book in his hands. He read over and over those well-selected volumes, enriching his mind with their finest passages.

Yet, despite all those exertions, Eric was far from being really happy or content. His one thought was deliverance from his strange situation, and he could not disguise from himself how dark his future looked. Ben, of course, could now be relied upon to the uttermost. But while his protection availed so long as they remained upon the island, matters would, no doubt, be different when the time came to leave the place. Then not only Evil-Eye, but all the other wreckers, would undoubtedly see to it that there was no fear of his becoming an informer, and placing them in peril of the law.

As the winter wore away, they often talked about going to Boston; and Eric gathered from their conversation that with the coming of spring they looked for a schooner sent out by confederates to take them and their booty home. This schooner now became the supreme object of his concern. In it he saw his best, if not, indeed, his only hope of deliverance. Many an evening when he seemed deep in his books he was, in reality, with strained ears and throbbing pulses, listening to the wreckers discussing their plans for the future. Tax his brains as he might, he could invent no satisfactory scheme.

More than once he tried to talk with Ben about the matter. But whether Ben did not wish to confess that he had no plan himself, or whether he thought it best not to excite uncertain hope, he always refused to talk about it, generally saying,—

"We'll see, my lad, we'll see. I'll do my best for ye, never you fear."

As spring drew near, signs of excitement and eager expectation became visible among the wreckers. They spent most of the clear days upon the highest hills, peering out across the waves in search of the schooner. They did not know just when to expect her. Indeed, had a date been fixed, they would not have been any better off, for they were without any means of keeping an account of the days, except by observing the sun and moon.

The days grew steadily longer and warmer, and yet no schooner appeared. Hope long deferred did not make the hot temper of the wreckers any more amiable, and Eric, worried as he was with his own troubles, found life harder than ever. Moreover, a new danger presently appeared.

The majority of the wreckers showed entire indifference toward him. He and his big dog were Ben's belongings, and so long as they got in nobody's way they were let alone. But when day after day and week after week slipped by, and the schooner did not arrive, the boy began to notice a change. Ugly, suspicious, threatening glances were cast upon him, and interchanged. Beyond a doubt, the peril of his position was alarmingly on the increase.

The explanation was simple enough. Like all men of their class, the wreckers were intensely superstitious, and the wily villain Evil-Eye, though indirectly, shrewdly seized upon the delay of the schooner to strike at Eric. He suggested to the men that the boy's presence was the cause of the vessel's non-appearance. He had brought them ill-luck, for not a wreck had come their way since his life had been spared. Now he was playing them another scurvy trick and, by some witchery, interfering with the carrying out of their plans.

The seed so craftily sown took root at once. Only the curious feeling, half-fear, half-admiration, that they held toward Ben saved Eric for a time from falling a victim to their superstition.

Even his influence would not have availed much longer, had not, one fine morning in May, the welcome cry of "Sail ho! sail ho!" rung out lustily from a watcher on the highest hill. Soon the broad sails of a schooner appeared.

Everything else was forgotten in the joy occasioned by this sight. But Evil-Eye, again foiled in his base designs, snarled savagely at Eric, and swore that he would have his own way yet.

The water being too shallow, the schooner hove-to about a mile from shore, and fired a gun to announce her arrival. But that was not necessary. All the inhabitants of the island were already on the beach to welcome her. Presently a boat was lowered, and three persons getting in, it was rowed swiftly ashore. The breakers were successfully passed with the aid of a number of the wreckers, who dashed into the surf, and drew the boat up high and dry upon the beach.

The new-comers were very heartily if somewhat roughly greeted. After the first excitement was over, Eric noticed they were looking at him curiously.

Evil-Eye whispered among them, whereupon they shook their heads as though to say,—

"Oh no, that can't be done. We're quite sure that won't do at all."

Eric's heart sank when he saw this, and rightly guessed its meaning. There seemed, at best, but two chances for him. He would either be left behind upon the island in helpless solitude, or be taken to Boston, and there got rid of somehow—in such a way that he could give no trouble to the wreckers. On the latter, surrounded although it was with uncertainties and dangers innumerable, he pinned all his hopes. It offered some faint chance of ultimate deliverance. But would they take him on board the schooner?

CHAPTER IX.

FAREWELL TO SABLE ISLAND.

Great was the bustle and excitement at the wreckers' quarters. The day happened to be particularly favourable for embarking—such a day, in fact, as might not come once in a month; and everything must be done to make the most of it. But the very beauty of the day gave evidence of approaching change. It was what the seafaring folk call a "weather-breeder," because such lovely days are always followed by storm.

None knew this better than the wreckers. They made all haste to transfer themselves and their booty to the schooner. In keen anxiety Eric watched the work going on. No one seemed to notice him, though several times he caught Evil-Eye regarding him with such a look of fiendish triumph as sent a shiver to his heart.

Ben, who had his own interests to care for, cheered him a little by clapping him on the back as he passed, and saying, in his most encouraging tone,—

"Keep up your heart, my lad. We'll manage it somehow."

But the removal of the booty was almost complete, and still he did not know his fate. Only another boat-load of stuff remained to be taken off, and in the boat that came for this were Ben, Evil-Eye, and the captain of the schooner. Eric stood near the landing-place with Prince beside him. He knew that his future hung upon what might be decided within a few minutes.

The boat was loaded, and the crew stood ready to launch her into the breakers. Now came the critical moment. How far the matter might have been discussed already Eric had no idea. He saw Ben draw the captain aside and engage him in earnest conversation, while Evil-Eye hung about as though he burned to put in a word.

His heart almost stopped beating as he watched the captain's face. Evidently he was not unmoved by Ben's arguments. His countenance showed he was wavering, and his opposition weakening.

With rising hope, Eric noted this. Evil-Eye saw it too, but with different feelings. He thought it time to interfere, and, drawing nearer, began, in a loud, half-threatening tone,—

"Say, now, captain—"

But before he could get out another word Ben wheeled round, his face aflame with anger. Rising to his utmost height, he drew a pistol from his belt, and pointing it straight at Evil-Eye's breast, roared out,—

"Hold that tongue of yours, *I* say, or I'll put a bullet through your heart before you can wink."

With a start of terror the ruffian shrank away from the giant who towered above him, and satisfied that he would not venture to interpose again, Ben resumed his talk with the captain. For a little longer the dialogue continued. What the arguments were that Ben used, or what inducements he offered, Eric did not learn until afterwards. But, oh! what a bound his heart gave when Ben left the captain and came toward him, his face so full of relief as to seem almost radiant.

"It's all right, my lad," said he, grasping him by the shoulder and pushing him toward the boat. "You're to come. Let's hurry up now and get on board."

Too overjoyed to speak, Eric hastened to obey, giving Ben a look of unspeakable gratitude as he clasped his hand with passionate fervour. Evil-Eye scowled terribly when the boy sprang into the boat, and dared only mutter his protests, for clearly enough Ben was in no mood for trifling, and the captain was evidently quite on his side.

Without waiting for an invitation, Prince promptly leaped in beside his young master, at which the men in the boat laughed, and the captain said good-humouredly,—

"Let him come too. He's too good to leave behind."

In a few minutes more, Eric, with a feeling of glad relief beyond all power of words to express, stood upon the schooner's deck and looked back at the island which for well nigh half a year had been his prison—almost his grave.

The low, broad, weather-beaten hut was easily visible. "How good God was to protect me there!" he thought, as he recalled the many scenes of violence he had witnessed. "I wonder what is to become of me. Poor father must have given me up for dead long ago. Shall I ever get to him?"

With many a "Yo! heave ho!" the sailors set about raising the anchor, the schooner's broad wings were hoisted to catch the breeze already blowing, and soon she was speeding away southward toward Boston.

They had just got well under way when, happening to glance around, Eric, who was standing in the bow enjoying the swift rush of the schooner through the foaming water, noticed a number of the wreckers and the crew gathered about the captain on the poop. They were examining something very carefully through his telescope. Following the direction of the glass, Eric could make out a dark object rising out of the water, several miles away on the port side. This was evidently the cause of the men's concern. Almost unconsciously he drew near the group, in order to hear what they were saying. The captain just then handed the telescope to Evil-Eye.

His face darkened with rage as he said, "It's one of those British brigs, and no mistake, and she's running right across our course. If we keep on this way we'll fall right into her clutches. Look you, Evil-Eye, and see if I'm not right."

Evil-Eye took the glass and looked long and carefully. It was clear enough that he came to the same conclusion as the captain, for one of his most hideous scowls overspread his countenance as he growled out,—

"It's the brig, and no mistake, and we're running straight into her jaws. We'll have to go about and sail off shore, captain."

At once the captain roared out his orders, and the sailors sprang to obey. There was a rattling of blocks, a creaking of booms, a fierce flapping of canvas. After a moment's hesitation in the eye of the wind, the schooner gracefully fell off, and was soon gliding away on the other tack, with the brig now almost directly astern.

Whatever doubt there may have been on board the brig as to the propriety of pursuing the schooner was dissipated by its sudden change of course; and, still distant though she was, a keen eye could make out that they were hoisting additional sails and making every effort to overtake the schooner.

There were yet three hours of daylight, and the brig was evidently a fast sailer. The schooner's chance of escape lay in keeping her well astern until night came on, and then, by a sudden change of course, slipping away from her in the darkness.

Every inch of canvas the schooner boasted was clapped on her, and, almost buried in foam, she rushed madly through the water.

Eric's first feeling, on seeing the brig, and the fear created among his captors, was of intense joy, and he watched its steady growth upon the horizon with eager anxiety. He did not notice the ominous looks cast upon him by Evil-Eye and others, until Ben, whose eyes seemed to miss nothing, drew him away to his former post near the bows, saying, in a deep undertone,—

"Come with me, lad. I want a word with you."

Ben's countenance showed that he was much troubled, and Eric, full of hope though he was at the near prospect of his own deliverance, could not help feeling as though it were very selfish of him, for it certainly meant that Ben would be placed in danger. He determined in his own mind that if the brig should capture the schooner, he would plead so hard for his kind rescuer that no harm would be done him.

"Will the brig catch up to us, Ben?" he asked eagerly. "Do you think it will?"

"It'll be a bad business for you, my lad, if it does," answered Ben, in an unusually gruff tone.

"Why, Ben, what do you mean?" asked Eric, in surprise.

"Mean what I say," retorted Ben. Then, after a moment's silence, he went on: "Captain says that brig's been sent from Halifax after us, and nobody else; and if she should catch us, you may be sure the wreckers ain't going to leave you round to tell the people on the brig all you know about them. Before the brig's alongside they'll drop you over the bulwark with a weight that'll prevent your ever showing up on top again."

At these words, whose truth Eric realized at once, his heart seemed turned to stone. And now, just as passionately as he had prayed that the brig might overtake them, did he pray that the schooner might keep out of its reach.

In the meantime, the two vessels were tearing through the water without much change in their relative positions.

Darkness was drawing near. As the sun went down, the change that the beauty of the morning foreboded took place. The sky grew cloudy, the wind blew harder, and there was every sign of an approaching storm.

As luck would have it, this state of affairs suited the schooner far better than the brig. With great exultation the wreckers noted that their pursuer was shortening sail. The square-rigged bark could not stand a storm as well as could the schooner.

"Hurrah!" the captain shouted gleefully. "They're taking in some of their canvas. They can't stand this blow with so much top-hamper. We'll show them a clean pair of heels yet."

And so it turned out. With bow buried in foam and decks awash the schooner staggered swiftly onward under full press of sail, although every moment the canvas threatened to tear itself out of the bolts. Before the darkness enveloped her the brig had disappeared behind, completely distanced. Everybody on board breathed more freely. Setting a course that, by a wide detour, would bring him in due time to Boston, the captain took satisfaction by cursing the brig for causing him the loss of a whole day at least.

That night Ben, for the first time, told Eric what had been arranged concerning him. On their arrival in Boston he was to be kept hidden in the hold until the time came for the sailing of a ship for England, about which the captain knew. He would be placed on board this ship as cabin boy. When she reached her destination he might make his way to his friends the best he could. By that time the wreckers (none of whom intended to return to Sable Island) would have disposed of their booty, and scattered beyond all possibility of being caught.

Ben did not add, as he might have done, that in order to effect this arrangement he had to bribe the captain, by turning over to him one-half of his own interest in the schooner's cargo.

After living in peril of death for so many months, this plan filled Eric's heart with joy. It might mean many more hardships, but it also meant return to those who were now mourning him as dead. He thanked Ben over and over again, assuring him he would never forget his wonderful kindness; and as Ben listened in silence there was a distinct glistening in the corner of his eye that showed he was not unmoved.

The storm blew itself out during the night, and was followed by a steady breeze, which bore the schooner along so fast that ere the sun went down on the following afternoon she was gliding up Boston Bay, looking as innocent as any ordinary fishing schooner. The anchor plunged with a big splash into the still water, the chain rattled noisily through the hawse-hole, and the voyage was ended.

Without delay a boat was lowered. The captain and Evil-Eye got into it, inviting Ben to accompany them, but he declined. He intended to watch over Eric until he should be taken to the English ship. The boat rowed off, and before it returned Eric was sound asleep.

He was awakened by the singing of the men as they toiled at the windlass, and the sullen rattle of the chain as it rose reluctantly link by link from the water. Then he heard the waves rippling against the bow, and he knew that the schooner was moving.

As he rightly guessed, she was making her way to her berth at the wharf. During all that day there was continual motion on the deck, and the boy imprisoned in the hold tried to while away the long hours by guessing what it meant, and what the sailors were about. Ben brought him a bountiful breakfast, dinner, and tea. He stayed only while Eric ate, and did not seem much disposed to talk. He could not say exactly when the English ship would sail, but thought it would be soon.

The schooner became much quieter by nightfall, for the majority of her crew had gone ashore. Soon there was perfect stillness; the vessel at times seemed to be completely deserted. There was a tower clock not far away which rang out the hours loudly, and Eric heard seven, eight, and nine struck ere he fell asleep.

How long he had slept he knew not, when he was aroused by two men talking in loud tones on the deck just above him. They were evidently the worse for liquor, and had fallen into a dispute about something. Presently one of them exclaimed,—

"It is there. I know it's there. I'll prove it to you."

CHAPTER X.

RELEASE AND RETRIBUTION.

Then came the sound of the fore-hatch being unfastened and lifted aside, and the light of a lantern flashed into the hold. Whatever the man sought, he soon found it; for he said triumphantly,—

"There, now! Do you see it? Didn't I say right?"

He drew the hatch back again, and with his companion went stumbling off to the cabin. As the hatch was opened, Eric shrank back into a corner, for he knew not what the man might be about. But when all was silent again, he crept to the spot underneath the hatchway, and looked up.

The instant he did so he saw something that caused his heart to give a wild bound. It was one little star shining brightly into his eye. The sailor had carelessly left the hatch unfastened and drawn a little aside.

The way of escape was there!

With bated breath and beating heart, Eric raised himself softly and pushed at the hatch. At first it would not budge, but on his putting forth more strength, it slid away a few inches, making no perceptible noise.

Little by little he pushed at it, until there was space enough for him to pass through. Then, with extreme caution, he lifted himself until he could survey the deck, and peered eagerly into the darkness to see if any of the men were about. There was no moon, but the stars shone their brightest; and as the boy's eyes were accustomed to the darkness, he could see fairly well.

It was easy for him to swing himself up on the deck. Then, crouched in the deep shadow of the foremast, he looked anxiously about him. Not a soul was in sight. Not a sound disturbed the still air. The black line of the wharf rose but a few feet above the bulwarks. Gliding noiselessly across, he finally got upon the rail, and thence, with an active spring, upon the wharf. He was free!

The wharf was as deserted and silent as the schooner's deck. Along one side was piled a line of casks and barrels, behind which he crept with the quietness of a cat until the tall warehouses were reached; then, straightening himself up, he moved more rapidly until he came out upon the street, which opened to right and left, leading away into the darkness—whither, he knew not.

Taking the right turning, he hastened on, resolved to appeal for protection to the first respectable-looking person he might meet. By the dim light of infrequent oil-lamps at the corners, he could make out that he was in a street of shops, taverns, and warehouses.

Some of the taverns were still open, but all the other buildings were closed. Very few persons were about, and as these all appeared to be seafaring folk he carefully avoided them, keeping in the shadow of porches and alley-ways until they passed. He was in a state of high excitement—his anxiety to find some safe refuge contending with joy at his escape from the wreckers' clutches.

He must have gone about a quarter of a mile, when, just as he approached a tavern that was still in full blast, the door suddenly opened, and a broad band of light fell upon the pavement, in the midst of which appeared Evil-Eye, roaring out a drunken song as he beckoned to others inside to follow him.

For an instant Eric stood rooted to the spot with terror. His limbs seemed powerless. Then, as quick as a squirrel, he darted into a dark alley at his right, and, trembling like an aspen leaf, waited for Evil-Eye to pass. The drunken scoundrel lingered for what seemed an hour of agony to the terror-stricken boy; but at length, being joined by his companions, staggered off toward the schooner. The boy, coming out from his retreat as soon as the coast was clear, made all haste in the other direction.

Following up the street, which turned and twisted in the puzzling fashion peculiar to Boston, he was glad to find it leading him to the upper part of the city; and after fifteen minutes' smart walking, he came out into a broad avenue, lined on both sides with handsome houses. Here he would surely meet with some one to whom he could safely tell his story.

Weary from excitement and exertion, he sat down upon a broad doorstep, which was in the shadow itself, but commanded a stretch of sidewalk illuminated by a street lamp. He thought he would rest there a while, and in the meantime some one would surely come along. Just as he sat down, the bell of a church-tower clock near by slowly tolled out the midnight hour.

"Oh, gracious! how late it is!" he sighed. "I do hope I shall not have to stay here all the night!"

A few minutes later he heard the sound of approaching steps. They were slow and deliberate, not those of an unsteady reveller. They came nearer and nearer, and then there emerged into the line of light the figure of a man, tall and stately, wrapped in a black dress, over whose cloak collar fell long locks of snow-white hair.

Not a moment did Eric hesitate. Springing from his hiding-place with a suddenness that caused the passer-by to start in some alarm, he caught hold of the ample cloak, and, lifting up his face to the wearer, said beseechingly, "Oh, sir, won't you help me?"

Quite reassured on seeing how youthful was this sudden disturber of his homeward walk, the gentleman looked down at the eager, pleading face, and, attracted at once by its honesty, put his hand kindly upon the boy's shoulder, saying,—

"Pray, what is the matter, my son? I will gladly help you, as may be within my power."

The grave, gentle words, with their assurance of protection, wrought a quick revulsion in poor Eric's feelings, strained as they had been for so long to their highest pitch. Instead of replying at once, he burst into tears; and his new-found friend, seeing that he had no ordinary case to deal with, took him by the arm, and soothingly said,—

"Come with me. My house is near by. You shall tell me your story there."

Directing his steps to a large house, in which lights were still burning, he led Eric into a room whose walls were lined with rows of portly volumes.

"Now, my son," said he, "be seated; and when you feel more composed, tell me your troubles. I am quite at your service."

With a delicious sense of security, such as he had not felt for many months, Eric sank into a big armchair, and proceeded to tell his strange story to the grave old gentleman before him. With intense interest and sympathy did Dr. Saltonstall listen to the remarkable narrative as it was simply related, putting in a question now and then when he wanted fuller details. As soon as the boy had finished, the doctor arose and again put on his hat and cloak.

"Master Copeland," said he, "this is a communication of the utmost importance, and it must be laid before the governor this very night, that immediate action thereon may be taken. I had but lately left his honour when, in God's good providence, I met you. We will go at once to his mansion. Haply he has not yet retired for the night."

Forthwith the two set out, and, walking rapidly, were soon at the governor's mansion. Fortunately he was still awake, and at once gave audience to his late visitors. Before him Eric rehearsed his story. The Honourable Mr. Strong listened with no less interest than had Dr. Saltonstall; nor was he less prompt in taking action. His secretary was summoned, and orders given for a strong posse of constables to be despatched without loss of time in search of the schooner.

Eric so fully described her that the finding of her would be an easy matter.

But while this was being arranged, a thought flashed into Eric's mind which filled him with great concern. Ben was, no doubt, upon the schooner now, and would be captured with the others. Would he not then share their fate, whatever that might be? And if so, would not Eric seem to be wickedly ungrateful if he made no effort to save him? Then there was also his faithful friend Prince, to whom both Ben and himself were so much indebted.

To think was to act. Going manfully up to the austere-looking governor, he put in a passionate plea for the big man and the dog, who had been such faithful protectors, and but for whom, indeed, he would not then be living. His honour was evidently touched by his loyal advocacy.

"Do not distress your mind, my lad," said he kindly. "I have no doubt we can find a way of escape for your friend. He certainly deserves consideration at our hands, and your noble Prince shall be carefully sought for."

The remainder of the story is soon told. The schooner was readily found. The wreckers, surprised in their bunks, proved an easy capture, and before daybreak all were safely locked up in jail. Prince was also found and restored to the delighted Eric, who now felt as though his cup of rejoicing was full. The trial of the wreckers excited widespread interest, and made Eric the hero of the hour. Ben, taking the advice of Dr. Saltonstall, turned state's evidence, and was released. But the other wreckers—from Evil-Eye to Black Joe—received the punishment they had so well merited.

In the meantime Dr. Copeland had been sent for, and, hastening to Boston, he had the supreme delight of clasping to his breast the boy whom he had all through the long winter been mourning as lost to him for ever. The meeting between father and son was touching. It seemed as though the doctor could never sufficiently assure himself that it was really his Eric who stood before him, browner of face and bigger of form, but otherwise unchanged by his thrilling experiences among the Wreckers of Sable Island.

THE END